When the Name Tree Sings

Karen Ginnane

Contents

One

Unwanted Plot Twist

Zain tugged at his clothes and frowned at the mirror. A scrawny figure wearing shorts that looked too baggy on skinny legs and an oversized t-shirt stared anxiously back at him.

He almost wished this new school had a uniform – though he would never say this out loud – so he wouldn't have to worry about how he looked every day.

A knock on the door, pushed open almost in the same moment.

"Dad! You could at least wait for me to say 'come in'," Zain said.

"I knocked, didn't I? And I need to leave, as do you." His dad looked at Zain with that familiar expression.

"I've told you before – clothes make the man. You can take on the world in a good shirt with a sharp collar and smart pants."

"I'm going to school, Dad."

"So what? Anything goes at that school. Some of those kids have coloured hair and wear ripped jeans – I think people would appreciate some smart clothes, Zain. You'd stand out! People might look at you twice."

Yeah, but some kids just own their looks, thought Zain. *They could wear a ball dress with running shoes and make it look exactly right.*

"Maybe I don't want anyone looking at me once, let alone twice," muttered Zain.

"What? Speak up, Zain! Don't mumble." His dad let out an impatient breath. "Look, I have to go. Your mum is still in bed, so make sure you get yourself organised and out the door in time, all right?"

"Is Mum okay?" asked Zain quietly, and this time Dad did not tell him to speak up.

Dad shrugged and turned away. "She's fine. Just don't be late, okay? Punctuality is important."

Zain left it too late to walk to school, so he had to catch the tram. He hated the packed morning tram, loud with jostling schoolkids from other schools nearby.

He swung his backpack off his shoulder and pushed his way onto the tram. Ben and Sam from his school were there with a bunch of other kids Zain didn't know. He nodded to Ben, who looked blankly at him before turning to laugh at something Sam had said. A girl – Ada? Ava? – shouted something to Sam about his new haircut, and Sam struck a pose and went red at the same time.

"Aw, you've made him blush!" shouted Ben, and everyone laughed, including Sam, who fluttered his eyelashes coyly. How was he always so cool about people laughing at him? The thought of all those eyes turning on Zain, waiting for a response – a *funny* response – made him prickle with anxiety. He would stand there awkwardly, oozing sweat and shame, and any laughter would be *at* him.

Zain pushed further up the tram, as far away as he could from the group. They were too busy bantering to notice Zain, so he could sit back and watch them wisecracking with each other, as if they were in one of the old movies Zain loved. He and his mum used to curl up together on the couch on Sunday afternoons with tea and biscuits, reciting the best lines word for word. They would compete with each other, making their delivery as dramatic as possible, but they had not done that for ages. Not since they had moved house, come to think of it.

Zain slouched off the tram at the school stop, channelling a cool-guy movie swagger as he shrugged his bag onto his back. Imagine being one of those guys, or one of the sassy actors who released one-liners with a perfectly raised eyebrow? Imagine not dissolving into panicky sweat whenever attention turned to you? Imagine actually *enjoying* it?

They had literacy first today, thank goodness. Ms Phillips was his favourite teacher – kind, calm, serious. Some of the kids said she was boring, but Zain loved her gentle attention, which gave him space to breathe, collect his thoughts, so that he could even answer questions in class. He never felt anxious around her. Ms Phillips was exactly how he needed this week to start.

He shuffled into the classroom with a couple of stragglers, not quite late, and took a seat at the side. Ms Phillips was not there yet, which was strange. She would usually be perched on the desk, watching them file in before she would clap her hands for quiet and the class would start.

The classroom buzzed with unsupervised energy until the door swung open again. The noise instantly dropped as a woman strode in, dressed in bright blue and green and jangling with bangles and long earrings. A quickly smothered titter rose at the back of the room as she dropped a pile of books on the desk and swung around to face the class. She had long black hair piled into a complicated bun with a big pink headscarf wound around her head, her eyes ringed with dark eye make-up. Her smile flashed around the classroom, and she spread her arms wide.

"Good morning, young people. I am Mrs Sharyar, and I am your teacher until the end of term."

Two

Mrs Sharyar

There was a long, awkward pause as the class stared back at the new teacher. It was Rose who broke the silence. "Where's Ms Phillips?" she asked.

"The estimable Ms Phillips has been unexpectedly called away. Life is not always predictable, my friends, but it means we have this gift of two weeks together, no?"

Zain glanced around and caught a side-eye from Ben, who rolled his eyes. "Why's she talking like that?" he muttered, and Zain rolled his own eyes in return.

"Right?" Zain murmured happily. He was usually the one the side-eye was about. Maybe having this teacher wouldn't be all bad, after all.

Mrs Sharyar picked up a green marker and turned to the whiteboard, scrawling big, sweeping letters that took up most of the board.

STORY

She underlined the word twice and turned back to the class, crossing her arms with a jangle and letting her eyes drift slowly across the room, looking hard at each of them in turn. When she reached Zain, he found he could not look away, even as his instincts screamed at him to. It was as if Mrs Sharyar's eyes held worlds that flashed before Zain. A crowded marketplace with bright spices and dusty camels. A laughing girl in a bright green scarf. A boat on a river at sunrise.

Mrs Sharyar moved on and the flashing images stopped. Zain blinked and heard a nervous laugh from one of the girls, Fiona. "What's she *doing*?" she asked, in not quite a whisper.

Zain knew exactly what Fiona meant. Looking at someone you didn't know like that was *weird*. And those images . . . could everyone else see them, too?

After an eternity of looking at every person in the class, the teacher flung out her arms again and flashed another huge smile.

"What beauties you all are!"

"You can't say that!" said Sophie, outrage loud in her voice. "A teacher can't make judgements on a student's physical appearance!"

Social Justice Sophie was always quickest to call out any hint of bigotry or bullying, and she usually made people see her point, but this teacher just smiled.

"Who said anything about physical appearance, my young firebrand? I'm talking about your souls. Your inner selves, with all your flaws, desires, fears and hopes. Your *humanity.*"

She turned back to the board as she said this and wrote "HUMANITY" in smaller letters in the space she had left under "STORY". She pointed to "STORY".

"What does this word mean?" she asked.

"It's another word for narrative," offered Jess.

"Yes. But I did not ask for a synonym. I asked for a meaning," said Mrs Sharyar, a gleam in her eye.

"It's – what – happens," said Sam, putting unnecessary emphasis on each word as if talking to a small child. He was rewarded with snorts of laughter from around the room.

"No, that is plot," said Mrs Sharyar blandly. "Anyone else?"

"Story is the telling of true or fictitious events in true or fictitious lives," chanted Rose.

"Again, that is plot," said Mrs Sharyar. "And I believe we might have Dr Google to thank for that response, hmm?" She gave another wink and the class laughed with her this time. Rose gave an "I'm busted" grin and closed the lid of her laptop sheepishly.

Zain could not stand teachers who relied on the class to fill in the gaps. What did she expect them to say? Everything that happened was a story. It was just *life.*

Suddenly, the teacher's eyes were on him, as if he had spoken out loud.

"Story is life. Story is everything. Now we're getting warm." She smiled approvingly.

Zain looked at Ben frantically. "Did I say that?" Zain whispered in panic, but Ben just shrugged and looked away.

"Story is what makes us human," continued Mrs Sharyar. "We tell stories to make sense of life. Without stories, we cannot be human. And I can guarantee that if I asked each of you to tell me what happened in this classroom today, you would each answer differently." She turned and underlined "HUMANITY". "These two words go together. You cannot have one without the other."

Maybe it had been just a coincidence, thought Zain, or maybe she was a mind reader, but at least he had not made a fool of himself in front of everyone.

"We will talk more about story. In fact, it is all we will talk about, as everything is story and story is life, as we have established." She gave a laugh. "Science is asking 'what if?' and then answering that question. History is simply all the stories that have happened before the stories we are living right now."

She's lost the class, for sure, thought Zain. *They have the attention span of a pencil.*

But the class was unusually quiet. They were all leaning forward, hanging on her every word. It was as if she had hypnotised them all. What was she saying now?

"... set you a task that you will deliver on Friday. I want each of you to tell a short story that is true to you. You can interpret that as you wish, but the heart of the story has to reflect your truth in some way." She held up a hand to forestall a question. "I won't give any more guidance than this. I want you to decide how to do this."

Well, that could be worse. Zain could write any old story and somehow make it about him. She could never know "his truth", anyway.

"Speaking of stories, we will now continue reading the book that Ms Phillips has been reading with you," said Mrs Sharyar.

Finally, she sounded like a normal teacher. This was the part of class Zain loved best. He flipped the book open as she sat down behind the desk.

"One more thing," she added. "There are two parts to this assignment. Not only will you give your story, but you will receive the stories of others. A story is a great gift, and in return you will accept each person's story with gentleness, understanding and gratitude."

"Wait – we have to tell our story to the whole class?" called Sam.

"Oh, yes. Storytelling always used to be oral, and, in this tradition, you will stand in front of the class and tell your story, as beautifully and expressively as you can."

Mrs Sharyar smiled as if all this was completely normal. As if it wasn't all of Zain's worst nightmares rolled into one. He stared at her in horror, but she was looking down at the page.

"And so, let us read," she said.

Three

Zain's Worst Nightmare

"End of term is meant to be *chill*," groaned Sasha.

The bell had released them from class with Mrs Sharyar, and the kids were jostling in the corridor.

"Are you crazy?" shot back Sam. "We get a chance to stand up and tell the class how great we are, and everyone has to listen *and* be thankful. 'The gift of my story, by Sam Moltoni.' I hope she gives me enough time," he said, furrowing his brow with mock worry.

"Well, it seems a waste of time to me," snapped Sophie. "How's that going to prepare us for exams?"

"I wonder if she's even qualified," said Fiona sniffily. "She doesn't look like any teacher I've seen before."

"Me neither," agreed Sophie. "Not to mention the way she talks."

"I thought she was cool," drawled Hope.

"Whoa, news flash! Hope likes a teacher!" shouted Ben.

Hope shrugged one laconic shoulder. "She was real," she said. "Don't freak out because she was a bit different, kids." She curled her lip before slouching down the hall, her hair the exact same shade of hot pink as her cut-off t-shirt.

Zain would give anything to have Sam's kooky confidence or Hope's terrifying cool. Whenever Sam opened his mouth, he was funny and normal, and Hope just didn't care what anyone thought. Whatever Zain said was stuttery and awkward, and he had never said more than a sentence in front of the whole class before.

For the rest of the day, he felt sick every time he thought of that homework. Maybe he would actually get sick, he thought hopefully. That seemed to be the only way out of this.

Zain looped around through the park on the way home. It took longer, but he liked the cool green away from the roaring road. He was less likely to encounter hordes of shouting schoolkids, and with his headphones on, he could pretend he was deep in his music. Anyway, he was in no rush to get home. Home meant facing Mum, and homework.

Zain didn't mind homework too much, normally. He could retreat to his room and also play games, ready to flip between windows on his laptop if a parent loomed. Today was different. Every time he thought of the task set by Mrs Sharyar, anxiety fizzed in his belly. There was no way he could stand up in front of the class and read a story he had written about himself. It was impossible.

Mum was home, as she always was these days. She had not found a job since they moved and seemed to have given up trying. At the beginning of term, she had been doing some drawings for herself, but she had not touched them for over a month now. Zain would give anything to be able to stay at home all day, but Mum did not look like she was enjoying herself much.

She was sitting in the garden, staring into space. She jumped when he opened the outside door. "Oh! Hi, Zainy," she said. "How was your day?"

He shrugged. "Okay."

Once upon a time she would have pestered him for more information, but now she just gave a distracted nod and said, "That's good."

He said, "Well, I'll just go and do some homework."

She looked up, as if vaguely surprised that he was still there. "That's good, sweetie," she said again, then turned back to stare at a different spot.

Zain had done science, maths and some essential gamer research by the time Dad got home at six o'clock. The rustle of bags sounded promising, and Zain poked his head around the door of the kitchen to see a pile of souvlakis with chips on the side.

"Great!" he said. Takeaway again. "I like this habit we're getting into."

Dad gave a grunt. "Don't get too used to it," he said. "It's just for now."

"Why now?" Zain asked, without thinking.

Zain saw Dad glance at Mum, who was slowly getting some plates out. Mum used to love cooking and would make most of the meals, even when they were both working. Zain realised now that she had not cooked a proper meal for ages. Dad had done the weekend cooking lately, and the week had been mostly leftovers and takeaway.

"Just until we get ourselves properly settled," said Dad. "Right, Orla? Any new jobs out there this week?"

Mum put down the plates and sat down with a sigh. "I haven't looked," she said. "Graphic design is so competitive."

"And you're good at it, Orla," said Dad firmly. "You've got to keep on getting out there."

"Mum's done lots of interviews but hasn't had much luck," said Zain quickly.

"You make your own luck, Zain. I've told you that many times," said Dad.

"Your dad's right," said Mum quietly. "I haven't applied for anything recently because – well, I hate graphic design."

They both stared at her. "But it's what you do, Orla," said Dad. "You've been so successful! I thought you loved it."

Mum shrugged. "Not any more. In fact, not for a long time. I've just been in the habit of it."

"So, what will you do?" asked Zain.

Mum shook her head. "I don't know." She pushed away her uneaten souvlaki and got up. "I think I'll have an early night. Goodnight."

Zain mumbled "goodnight" as Mum left the room, then Zain and Dad finished their food in a silence that was somehow very loud.

Four

Things Can Get Worse

The next day, Mum was quieter, and Dad's face was tighter. Takeaway again, but now it was no longer exciting. Zain looked at the curry Dad brought home for dinner, and at his mum barely touching the food on her plate. He hoped Dad would not start one of his pep talks again.

Dad cleared his throat. "I spoke to our neighbour today on the way home from work," he said. "Her name's Ellen. Very nice woman, very involved with the local community. There's lots of volunteer work around."

Mum poked a piece of paneer and said nothing.

"She said there is a walking group she's part of," Dad continued. "Also, she does yoga. A new hobby would be good for you, Orla."

Mum looked up. "I don't need a hobby, Joe."

"You need something!" Dad said. He put down his fork and looked at her. "Ellen said she hadn't even met you yet. She told me that she left you a note asking you over and you haven't responded. I'm sorry to say this, Orla, but you're not helping yourself. Other people can't help you if you won't make an effort!"

Mum pushed her plate away and got up. "I'm tired, Joe. I'm going to bed."

"Orla, I'm not asking for much," said Dad. His voice was very quiet, but somehow it was worse than if he had shouted. "I'm working all hours in this new job, and all you have to do is get to know people. You just have to make an effort." Dad shook his head. "I don't know how you can be so tired. You don't *do* anything."

The words hung horribly in the air and Zain's stomach twisted, but Mum just turned and walked away. The bedroom door clicked shut behind her.

Zain stared at the rice and dal on his plate, all appetite gone. Dad let out a loud breath and turned back to the food on his plate, attacking it as if it were the enemy. He chewed vigorously before jabbing a finger at Zain.

"Nobody hands you anything on a plate in this world, Zain. You have to fight to succeed. Understand?"

Zain nodded silently. He understood all right. He understood that both he and Mum were a disappointment to Dad, and as much as Zain wished he didn't care, he did.

Dad had already gone to work by the time Zain was up the next day, which was a relief. The black, twisting ball in Zain's belly churned every time he thought of Dad's face, those words, and his mum's awful silence. There was no sign of Mum, again.

He stepped out of the house and the tightness in his shoulders relaxed. He felt like he could breathe again. He had time to walk to school today, looping around through the park.

He got to the crossing near the school and saw Sam and Ben clowning around. Sam had one arm up in the air like a town crier.

"Hear this, hear this!" he cried. "The magnificent story of one Sam Moltoni, the great joy of his parents' lives! The skies lit up with fireworks and the flowers wept with joy on the day of his birth. He was –"

Ben tackled Sam from behind, one arm slung around his neck. "Stop, stop! My ears are bleeding!" shouted Ben. The two boys fell around laughing.

Zain had managed to push Mrs Sharyar's task aside, but Friday was getting ever closer – and he still had nothing. How could it be Wednesday already?

The day passed too quickly, and before he knew it, he was trudging home again. He stopped to listen at his front door, but the only sound was his key turning in the lock. His heart sank. A silent house might mean his mum was having another nap, or that she was sitting there twisting her fingers and staring into space. It would not mean she was on a shopping trip or seeing friends. If only.

The door swung open. There was mail shoved through the letterbox, as there had been when Zain had left. The single running shoe lying on its side, smack bang in the middle of the doorway to the kitchen, had not changed position.

"I'm home, Mum!" he called brightly. If he kept acting normal, his mum might remember how to be herself again. He dropped his bag with a thud on the ground. "Mum?"

Her bedroom door was shut tight. He tapped on her door. "Mum?"

Silence. He knocked loudly. "Mum, are you asleep?"

Still nothing. He pushed the door open and breathed in the stale fug of an airless room. She used to be such a fresh air freak, but now the windows were all closed. Zain switched on the light. "Mum, it's after four o'clock."

She rolled over to look up at him blearily and rubbed her face. "Are you going to school?" she mumbled.

"I've just come home. It's the afternoon."
An awful realisation was dawning on Zain. She was wearing her pyjamas. "Mum – did you get out of bed today?"

She looked up at him, eyes dull. He swallowed down the black dread creeping up from his belly and patted her hand. "I'll make you a cup of tea. You'll feel like getting up then. Okay?"

They were out of milk. He made her a black Earl Grey and took it in to her with a stale biscuit.

He put the cup and saucer carefully in her hands and sat at the foot of her bed. "Mum, you have to get up. We need some milk; we should go to the shops."

She sipped her tea and sighed. "I'm just so tired, Zain. I'm sorry." She let her head fall back against the bedhead and closed her eyes, as if the act of lifting the cup had been too much.

"It's okay, Mum," said Zain quickly. "I can go, I'll take your wallet. You can get dressed while I'm gone. Dad's home soon."

They both knew how Dad would react if he came home to see Mum like this. She nodded without opening her eyes.

"I'll get some bread and we can have baked beans on toast. We can watch something on TV, if you want." At least they wouldn't be eating takeaway again.

To his horror, he saw a tear trickle from beneath Mum's closed right eyelid. "You're a good boy, Zainy. I should be a better mum. A proper mum."

He jumped up off the bed. "You just need something to eat. I'll be back soon, when you're dressed."

He could not get out of the room fast enough, his chest swelling as if it would burst as he grabbed her wallet from the bag hanging from the doorknob and ran back out the front door.

Five

Home Life

Dad came home earlier than expected.

Zain and Mum were watching *Charade*, one of their favourite old movies. Zain had been watching his mum for the flicker of a smile at the lines they both loved, and he had finally caught one – but in the next moment, they both heard the key in the door.

Zain grabbed the plates with smears of cold baked beans and ran for the kitchen – but too late. He almost collided with Dad as he came through the doorway, work satchel still slung over his shoulder. Zain saw the scene as Dad would: Mum in her unwashed tracksuit with still-wet hair from a shower, Zain guiltily clutching plates of the food Dad hated most, watching movies in the afternoon on a school day. The house a mess around them.

Dad's eyebrows were nearly at the top of his forehead. "Baked beans for dinner? At –" he checked his watch, "– 5:33 pm?" He made a show of looking around. "I'm relieved to see you haven't saved a plate for me."

"Hi, Dad," said Zain brightly. "It's more of an after-school snack. It was my idea." He edged around his dad and bolted for the kitchen. Dad was never scary, but Zain hated the way his whole face went sad and droopy. The disappointment was almost worse than anger.

Zain scraped the plates, pretending not to watch as Dad sat down next to Mum. Dad lowered his voice, but the big, open-plan space meant Zain could still hear every word. Dad was asking Mum about her day.

Don't tell him, don't tell him, don't tell him, Zain chanted in his head. *Don't let that big black cloud of disappointment hang over the house again.*

But Mum was shaking her head. "I don't know why, Joe," he heard her whisper. "I just couldn't get up. I'm so tired today."

Dad put his hand on Mum's knee. "Are you sick?" He sounded worried.

Mum shook her head again. "No, I had my physical check-up recently. It's just this tiredness."

Dad sighed. "Orla, you should do some exercise. You feel tired because you sit around all day." He pulled his hand away and pressed his lips together as if trying to hold some words back. They came out anyway. "I really don't know what else I can do. You don't want to work; you don't want to not work. I don't know what you want any more."

Mum had been looking down at her lap all this time, but now she raised her head. "I don't know either, Joe." Her voice was so soft next to Dad's. "But I just can't do that job any more. I don't care about corporate logos, about packaging for frozen peas."

Zain finished with the plates. He was halfway to the doorway when Dad's attention swivelled his way. "I've got homework to do," said Zain quickly.

"Not so fast," said Dad. He gestured towards the TV. "What have we discussed about the importance of a study routine in school? Get behind now and you'll struggle later."

"I'm going now, Dad."

"You do homework as soon as you get home, to leave time for exercise and an early night. And a decent meal," he added. He got to his feet suddenly. "Have you enrolled in the soccer team yet?"

Zain shuffled his feet.

"Has he, Orla?" His mum shook her head and shrugged in a defeated sort of way.

Dad took a deep breath. "I can't work and hold everything together here as well," he said, too quietly. "I can't be the only grown-up in this house."

Mum flinched as if the words had stung, but Dad was already on his way out the door. "I'm going to the gym, and then I'll eat something out." He turned to gaze at them both with that disappointed look. "I just don't know what else to do."

The front door slammed, and the house quivered.

Six

Arabian Nights

Mum was very quiet after Dad left. She sat staring at a spot on the wall as Zain turned the TV off.

"He's right, Zainy," she said. "I'm no role model for you."

The tone of her voice made a chill run through him. "Don't say that, Mum."

"Go and do your homework, Zain." He hesitated, but she turned and gave him a smile. "I'm fine. Really. Go on."

So Zain went, but he kept an ear out over his maths exercises, and after a while he heard the door to her bedroom quietly close. He sighed. Maybe she did just need to rest. She might feel better for it in the morning.

Dad came back after a few hours. Zain had finished his homework for the day, but made sure he was bent studiously over a book when Dad tapped on his door and entered in the same moment.

"Come in," said Zain, unnecessarily. He looked up and said, "Oh. Okay."

"A present for you," said Dad, spinning a soccer ball expertly on one finger. "We can have a kick around in the park, get your skills up until you get on a team."

He smiled at Zain, who was so relieved to see his change of mood that he nodded and said, "Great!" and almost meant it.

"Tomorrow after school, then. I'll start early and be back by five o'clock," said Dad. He looked at the book Zain was holding. "How's the homework?"

"Yeah, good," said Zain. "Maths and history done; this is literacy." He waved the book.

Dad peered at the title. "Never heard of it. What else are you learning in literacy?"

"We have to tell a story," said Zain without thinking, and then wished he hadn't as his belly clenched tight in anxiety again. Dad snorted.

"Sounds like a waste of good learning time to me. Fairy tales are for little kids." He let the ball spin off his finger towards Zain, who grabbed at it but missed. Dad sighed. "Get an early night and we'll start fresh tomorrow."

Zain did get an early night, but he lay in bed tossing and turning for so long that his morning alarm was a nasty shock. Dad had already left by the time Zain was dressed and in the kitchen. There was no cereal left, so he put some bread in the toaster and poured some juice.

Mum was nowhere to be seen. She might have gotten up early. Perhaps she was walking around the block right now or doing a lap of the park. She used to love those big trees, full of brightly coloured birds. Zain knew he was kidding himself, his hands making a cup of coffee even as he imagined that.

He took the cup to the bedroom door and tapped. "Made you a coffee, Mum," he said. He left the door open so he could navigate the dimly lit room, putting the cup carefully by her bed. He opened the blinds with a clatter. Daylight would make it all normal in here.

She flung one arm over her eyes as if he had shone a spotlight into her face. "Shut the blinds, Zainy. Too tired."

"No, Mum. It's time to get up. It's daytime, you can't just keep sleeping." Little bursts of panic started fizzing in his belly and chest. "Shall I call the doctor?"

She mumbled something else, and he leaned forward. "What did you say?"

She mumbled again, and the panic fizzes got bigger. He glanced at the clock on Dad's side of the bed. *8:28*. School started in twelve minutes. It was Mrs Sharyar for first lesson today. There was no point in rushing out now. He would never make it, and walking in late and having to explain was far worse than not turning up at all.

And anyway, the thought of his bangled teacher had given him an idea. "Mum, we're going to read stories together. Right now."

He jumped up and ran out to the bookcase in the hallway, which contained Mum's most precious books. He ran one finger over the glossy, embossed spines and stopped on the one he knew she loved the most, as much for its beautiful pictures as for the words: *Arabian Nights: Tales from the Thousand and One Nights*. He took it down and flipped through it, remembering these vivid, lush illustrations from his childhood, when his mum would read to him.

Well, now it was his turn. He took the heavy book into the bedroom and arranged the pillows behind her head. He sat down beside her. "Remember this, Mum? Look at these pictures! You're as good as this artist, you should do some drawing again."

He was rewarded with a faint snort, but her eyes were on the richly coloured pictures of winged horses, people riding elephants through banana trees and rooms full of vivid carpets, wall hangings and jewels. Zain scanned the blurb on the first page, which his mum had never read to him before.

The "Tales from the Thousand and One Nights" are said to have been originally told by Scheherazade to her husband, evil King Shahryar, who planned to do away with her the day after they married. The king met his match in Scheherazade, who told him a story every night, always stopping at a moment of cliffhanging excitement in order to keep herself alive.

Scheherazade's world is one in which anything is possible – young men are turned half to stone, the earth opens up and swallows the unwary, spells and potions make dreams come true or bring disaster, and magical beings appear from nowhere to determine an individual's fate.

"Scheh – Shah – Sherah – whatever, her world sounds good to me," said Zain, flicking through to choose a story. "Though I think you changed the words a bit when you read them to me when I was little!"

"Sheh-hair-uh-zahd," said Mum, sounding a bit croaky. "That's how you say it."

Zain looked at her in surprise. Was he imagining it, or did her eyes look brighter already? "I'll call her Shez to save time, okay?"

"Okay," said Mum, and laughed. His mum *laughed.*

With a warm glow in his chest, he said, "Let's start with 'Ali Baba and the Forty Thieves'."

Shez could definitely work magic.

Seven

She Wouldn't, Would She?

It was funny, but for the rest of the day, Zain kept on seeing things about Shez, having never heard of her before.

Zain had eventually set off to school at his mum's insistence, after reading several stories. On the way, he heard an old couple talking about a famous Cafe Scheherazade that used to be in a seaside suburb, where Jewish refugees would come to share their stories. And then, when he got to school, he quite literally ran into Mrs Sharyar coming out of the classroom into the corridor, knocking a piece of paper from the pile of books she was carrying.

"Sorry," he mumbled in embarrassment, grabbing the leaflet as it fell. It was for a performance by the local town orchestra, called

"Scheherazade". He stared at it in surprise. "There are 1001 reasons to fall in love with this music," he read.

"The name tickled me," said Mrs Sharyar, smiling at him. She reached out a hand. "I simply had to hear music dedicated to the greatest storyteller of all time."

He handed it back to her and said, "I was reading her stories to Mum. That's why I'm late."

Why had he told her that?

"Aha. Your mother is ill in bed?" she asked.

"Yes," he said, again without meaning to. Whatever was he thinking, blurting out his private life?

"I would love to meet your mother, Zain. Perhaps we could meet up when she's feeling better, and have a chat?"

"Um," he said. "Well, I mean . . ." he stammered, trying desperately to think fast. How did she know his mother was in bed? Not that she was ill. Just tired.

"I have to go to class," he blurted out, and turned to run. It was true – he was about to miss the start of his sports class, and the thought of the sarcastic greeting he would get from Mr Walker if he walked in late made him sprint.

He spent the lesson in a blur of anxiety. Mrs Sharyar wouldn't *actually* want to meet his mum, would she? Maybe it was against the rules, he thought hopefully – some sort of invasion of privacy, a breach of student–teacher contact guidelines or something.

Wait a minute. She didn't know where he lived. Zain sat bolt upright, relief sweeping over him. That was it! He could just not give her the address, and there was no way the school would give out private information about a student. He was safe.

By the time the last bell rang, Zain had almost forgotten about his fright from the morning. It had been a good day, for him. He had hung out with another student at lunch-time. Well, talked to. Well, exchanged a couple of words in the canteen line with. But they had been friendly words, and the other kid had even laughed at something Zain had said. The warm glow of that moment stayed with Zain for the whole afternoon.

He hoisted his bag on his shoulder and set off for home. Hopefully Mum would be up and about this afternoon. She had been better than he had seen her for ages when he had left this morning, after they had lost themselves in an hour or so of stories and colourful pictures. She had gotten dressed and even waved to him as he left. He smiled to himself as he waited for the lights to change at the pedestrian crossing near the school.

"Share the joke, Zain!" called John, the crossing supervisor who knew everyone's name and always had a grin and a greeting. Zain blushed and shook his head as John winked at him. "Nice to see you grinning, anyway," John said kindly. Zain put his head down and hurried across. John always embarrassed him, but in a nice way. He turned to go down the laneway opposite the crossing, John's banter in full flow behind him.

And then: "Hello, Mrs Sharyar! Off to relax after work?"

Zain froze on the spot.

"Greetings to you, John!" called his teacher. "Isn't it a beautiful afternoon? Ah, Zain! I thought I'd missed you."

Zain's heart plummeted into his shoes. The impulse to bolt was almost overwhelming – but that would be even more embarrassing. He turned, slowly, to see Mrs Sharyar bustling towards him. The last thing he wanted was to talk to Mrs Sharyar about his mum. He could feel the curious glances of other kids flicking towards him.

Zain gave a forced smile and turned in resignation, walking up the laneway. Mrs Sharyar was just behind him, chatting to two of the girls she taught. They turned the opposite way to Zain, and Mrs Sharyar waved goodbye before falling into step with Zain.

"You worry about your mother, don't you, Zain?" Her voice was so soothing, and her eyes were so kind that he found himself nodding. "And you worry about what others think of you. It's a lot of worry for such a young man."

He looked at her quickly, but she wasn't laughing at him. She went on. "Your mother's story, and yours, are both in a moment of crisis. All stories have this, you know. But I predict that there will soon be a twist."

Before Zain could think of how to reply to that, she changed the subject, to his relief. "Look at the size of that date palm! Almost as big as the old ones I grew up with. I used to love eating fresh dates in the morning as a girl. Labneh, honey, dates and coffee. Perfection!"

Eight

Under the Name Tree

Mrs Sharyar told Zain such vivid stories about her childhood in Baghdad that by the time they had crossed the park, he was vaguely surprised to find himself still in his own neighbourhood. He was even more surprised to hear a familiar voice call his name.

"Zainy!"

He turned to see his mother walking along the running track, her face pink with exercise. She smiled and he grinned back, forgetting his teacher for a moment to marvel at the sight of his mother out and about.

"Hi, Mum," he called.

"I had the strongest impulse to come to the park just now," she said. "I'm not sure what came over me."

Her eyes flicked past him with a questioning look. Too late, he realised the thing he had been dreading had happened. How was his quiet mum going to respond to this strange, talkative teacher with her flowing, colourful clothes, her jewellery and headscarves, her thick eye make-up?

Well, he was about to find out. "Um, this is my teacher, Mrs Sharyar," he said, feeling awkward. This was such a weird situation.

Mrs Sharyar extended a hand to his mother. "Mrs Agassi, it's a pleasure to meet the mother of the remarkable Zain."

Remarkable? His mother reached out her own hand tentatively, as if she had forgotten how to do this, but she was smiling. "Hello, Mrs Sharyar," she said.

Mrs Sharyar shook his mother's hand, bangles jingling vigorously. "I'm delighted to meet you. I have a very small gift, really nothing at all."

His teacher reached inside the big bag hanging from her shoulder, took out a wrapped box and handed it to his mother. "These are excellent with coffee," she said.

Mum looked surprised but took the box. "Thank you. Oh, and please, call me Orla," she said, as if remembering herself.

"And you must call me Zade," said Mrs Sharyar, pronouncing it to rhyme with *card*. "It's my favourite nickname. I have had many, in a life as long as mine!" She chuckled and touched a finger lightly to the laughter lines around her eyes.

A pause, and then his mother asked, hesitantly, as if she had forgotten what the correct etiquette was, "Would you like – to come home for a coffee?"

"I would *love* a coffee," declared Mrs Sharyar.

Mrs Sharyar stepped onto their front porch, looking as out of place as a parrot on a tram in her vividly coloured clothes. She followed Mum inside, hands clasped in delight, looking around as if she was in a palace.

"A lovely home you have, Orla. And your garden, with these mature trees! How fortunate you are."

"How do you take your coffee, Zade?" asked Mum.

"Short and black, please. I will prepare the kleicha if you would be kind enough to pass me a plate?"

Mrs Sharyar stood at the kitchen island, chatting easily as she laid little pastries on his mother's cake platter, turning their quiet kitchen into a lively and warm space. She broke open a little cake and held a piece out to Zain and his mother. "Try these! The best kleicha you will ever taste."

Zain took it and sniffed, his head filling with heady, delicious scents of cinnamon, cardamom, rosewater, coriander and sesame. "They look like maamoul," he said, and Mrs Sharyar nodded.

"Yes, they are similar – but much better." She gave that expert wink again.

His mother had already bitten into hers. "Oh!" she said with her mouth full. "The dates! The spices! They are so – oh!" she said, and took another bite, her expression blissful as she chewed.

"They are guaranteed to bring words to the lips, are they not?" said Mrs Sharyar with satisfaction. She glanced outside and picked up the plate and her coffee. "We shall eat them under that magical she-oak tree. Zain, could you get the door and bring some chairs?"

Zain did as she asked, bringing over two chairs and a small table and helping Mrs Sharyar arrange them under the fronds that always made him think of long hair hanging down. The two women sat down, and Mrs Sharyar gave a contented sigh.

"The best place to talk is underneath trees, and this one is special. Do you know why? According to some wise Elders of these lands, this tree is a name tree. It holds the names of everyone who passes underneath it." She looked at Zain's mother. "All trees hold stories, but this one sings them when the wind passes through. It is a comfort, is it not, to know our stories are all kept safe in this tree? Even if we think we have forgotten them ourselves?"

His mother was staring at Mrs Sharyar, and there was colour in her cheeks that Zain had not seen there for a long time. Zain strongly suspected that his teacher was not quite in touch with reality, but if her crazy words brought his mother to life – well, that was all that mattered.

"I have to do some homework," he said, and ran inside.

It was impossible to concentrate on maths with Mrs Sharyar in the garden, and Zain kept creeping out of his room to peek at the alien sight of his mother and teacher sitting together under the tree. He was peering at them for the third time when the sound of the key in the front door announced Dad's arrival home. With a start, Zain remembered the soccer ball and their planned kick around. Had that conversation really only happened last night? It felt like another lifetime.

Dad called from the hallway, "Ready for some soccer, Zain?" He came into the kitchen and his expression changed. "What's that?"

Dad went over to the box of pastries and took out one of the cakes that had not made it onto Mrs Sharyar's platter. His face wore a strange expression. "These remind me of the kolompeh my grandmother used to make," he muttered, as if somewhere else. He lifted it to his nose and sniffed. "They even smell like Iran." He took a bite and chewed slowly, his eyes closed for what seemed like an eternity. He swallowed and sighed as he opened his eyes again. "I've never tasted anything quite like this, but somehow it also has the taste of home."

Zain was not used to such words coming from the mouth of his rational accountant father, and didn't know what to say. He blurted out, "Mum's talking to my teacher under the tree."

Dad blinked and seemed to come out of his trance. "Really?"

Zain gestured and they both looked at the two women leaning forward in intense conversation. This time, it was Mum who was doing the talking. "Yes, really."

Zain and Dad watched in silence for a long moment, and then Dad moved to the open door. Instead of going outside, as Zain expected him to do, he gently pulled it shut. "I think now's a good time to kick a ball around, Zain," he said quietly. "Let's not disturb them."

Zain nodded. "I'll go and get changed."

For once, kicking a soccer ball around with his dad felt like exactly the right thing to do.

Nine

Truth Telling

When Zain and Dad returned home, hot and sweaty after an hour and a half of soccer, Mrs Sharyar had left. The little table and chairs were still under the tree, but the pastries had been put away and the plates tidied, surfaces wiped down. Mum was sitting in front of the TV, watching with a smile playing around her lips. She pressed pause when she caught sight of them.

"You're very lucky to have Mrs Sharyar as your teacher, Zain," said Mum. "She really likes you."

Zain and Dad both stared at Mum. Dad went and sat down next to her, his face split in a grin. "It's good to see you looking so well, Orla," he said. "Your teacher should come over more often, Zain!"

"She has a way with words," said Mum. "Her stories took me out of my head and into other worlds." She paused. "I felt – *connected*."

"Is this your storytelling teacher, Zain?" asked Dad. Zain nodded and Dad grunted. "I'm glad her stories made you feel better, Orla. Storytelling certainly has its place, with children and sick people."

"No, Joe. Stories are for everyone. Stories are as important as anything," said Mum firmly. "Perhaps more important. They teach you how life works."

Dad snorted and waved at the TV. "They are entertainment. What useful things do stories teach you about life?"

Mum looked thoughtful. "How important it is to hold onto dreams. To know who you are, even when everyone else wants you to be different." She looked at Dad. "We all need to know that, Joe. Don't we?"

Dad was silent for a long moment, before clearing his throat and getting to his feet. "Well. I have to have a shower," he said, and left the room.

Mum turned the TV off. "I'm ready for bed," she said with a yawn. Zain's heart sank.

"It's only 6:30, Mum. What about dinner?" he asked.

She rubbed her eyes. "I ate so much kleicha," she said sleepily. "And it's been a big day. Night, Zain." She got up, tousled his head and went to her room.

The next morning, Zain shot upright as soon as his alarm squawked, adrenalin pumping through every cell as he remembered. Today was Friday! And he still had no idea what his story was.

Maybe he had a sore throat. He almost definitely had a sore throat. He cleared his throat experimentally. And a fever, he could feel the sweat running down his side. He coughed a few times and sighed loudly. It took a couple of attempts, but eventually Dad came to his door. "Zain, why are you still in bed?"

"I feel ill," Zain croaked. "I should stay here in case I spread germs. Can you sign me off school today?"

Dad came in and bent over Zain, laying a palm on his forehead. "Hmm. Feels all right to me. Stick your tongue out," he commanded.

Zain did so and Dad peered down his throat. "No redness."

"I ache all over," said Zain hopefully.

"That's because you trained for the first time last night," said Dad unsympathetically. "You're fine. Up you get."

"But I'm all sweaty!" protested Zain.

"Then have a shower," said Dad.

"And I feel sick," Zain added.

"You always do when you get nervous. Just a minute. What's going on at school today, Zain?" asked Dad suspiciously.

"Nothing."

"Isn't today the story day, Zain?" called Mum from the hallway.

Of all the days for Mum to decide to get up in the morning, why did it have to be this one? Zain pulled the doona over his head and groaned until Dad yanked it off.

"Up! No hiding in bed. If something scares you, face it," said Dad. "Ridiculous idea, anyway, telling stories in class."

In that matter, at least, Zain agreed with Dad one hundred per cent.

Zain stood in the corridor outside the classroom and took a deep, wobbly breath. He could not put it off any longer. He sidled inside and found a seat towards the back. Mrs Sharyar was already there, writing something vigorously on the board, bangles jangling as she did so. She turned and gestured dramatically to the words.

STORIES SAVE LIVES!

"Stories make sense of lives; they shine light on lives, and they save lives. Yes, truly." Her gaze swept the classroom. "These stories might be funny or sad or even very ordinary, but it doesn't matter, as long as they are true. And truth can take different forms." She paused, her expression serious. "What we need to remember is that everyone is struggling with something. Every – single – person. And so, we will be kind. We will be the soft cushions that these stories will land upon. We will treat them as the precious gifts they are. None of them will be perfect, and that is perfectly human." She smiled. "Great storytellers are made by practice, and we start today."

Mrs Sharyar went to the desk and leaned against it. "Are we all sitting comfortably? Good. Now, each story must take no more than four minutes, so that we have time to hear them all. Do we have a volunteer for the first story?"

Ten

The Terrible Thing Happens

A long silence filled with side glances and shuffles was broken unexpectedly by Hope. Not confident Sam, not popular Rose, but scornful Hope. For a second, Zain forgot his churning belly at the surprising sight of Hope willingly making her way to the front of class.

Without waiting for an introduction, she began. "I acknowledge the Wurundjeri people, the traditional custodians of this land, who have been telling stories here for thousands of years. I pay my respects to their Elders, past and present. This land is unceded and we are neither guests nor invited." She paused and stared fiercely around the room. "My story is about not belonging on the land I was born on."

The class was silent as Hope went on. She talked about finding out the history of the land she grew up on. "I thought it was beautiful when I was a child, and I still do. But then I found out it was also a battleground. Ever since, I've heard the ghosts here." She looked at Mrs Sharyar and her eyes were bright. "They still haunt me today, so my story is a ghost story. We must know these ghost stories because they are also the stories of everyone else who lives here."

The class was silent for a long moment until Mrs Sharyar clapped. "A powerful story, Hope, and wise words." She pressed one hand to her chest and held Hope's gaze. "Thank you for sharing your story."

She turned back to the class. "Sam, you next. I believe you are well prepared?" She gave a wink and the class laughed, breaking the mood.

Mrs Sharyar knew what she was doing, as Sam's funny story cleared the air. One after another she chose storytellers, somehow judging it perfectly so that sad followed funny, serious balanced light-hearted and awkward storytellers were put next to kind ones. Some kids told their stories together, standing side by side for moral support.

In spite of the panicky queasiness in his stomach, Zain felt something happening. The air was bubbling with a kind of energy and aliveness. There *was* something about sharing stories, he realised, and every story was listened to respectfully and applauded. Perhaps, just perhaps . . .

"Zain?" With a start, he realised Mrs Sharyar had been talking to him. "Will you share your story?"

It was as if the room collapsed onto Zain's chest. He could not breathe. Blood hummed in his ears and faces swam around him. He stared at Mrs Sharyar in desperation. His mouth opened but nothing came out. His heart thudded painfully against his ribs, and he heard himself let out a grunt. In the next moment, Mrs Sharyar was crouched in front of him, hand on his head.

"Breathe, Zain. All you have to do is breathe," she said softly. "In. Out. Here, drink some water." Somehow a water bottle was in front of him. He lifted it, drank shakily and put it down. Then Mrs Sharyar's arm was under his elbow, and she was saying something to the class. She was leading him out, down the hallway, into another room, and settling him in a chair. He closed his eyes and concentrated on breathing.

When he opened them, Mrs Sharyar had gone and Ms Donati, the school counsellor, was holding a paper cup out to him. He took it and gulped down the tangy liquid.

"Rehydration salts. You're in sickbay, Zain. Your teacher will be back shortly to see how you are," said Ms Donati. She leaned forward. "It seems you had an anxiety or panic attack," she said kindly. "Has this happened before?"

He shook his head, shame flushing hot in his cheeks. He had humiliated himself in front of the whole class without saying a word. Only he could achieve that, he thought bitterly.

"It's nothing to be ashamed of, Zain. It's more common than you might think," Ms Donati said. "We can help you manage these in future."

He looked at his feet and said nothing.

"Zain, looking after your mental health is no more embarrassing than having to brush your teeth," she said firmly.

The bell for the end of the day blared, and the corridors filled with feet and voices. Easy laughter, jokes, shouts. The relaxed chatter felt like a language he had never learned. Mrs Sharyar's face appeared in the glass, and she pushed open the door. Behind her Zain could see curious glances from classmates.

"Okay, Zainy boy?" called Sam. "Hope you're feeling better." Zain flicked him a glance, but there was no sign of the usual smirk.

Ben was beside him, and the concern in his eyes looked real. "Hey, Zain, take it easy, dude. Okay?"

Other classmates leaned in to call words of encouragement or sympathy, as if it was no big deal, as if he had not just made a total fool of himself. As if he was not a social pariah.

Mrs Sharyar was talking to Ms Donati. She turned to Zain. "It's home time. You can go home if you feel well enough, Zain. We'll arrange a support plan with the school next week."

When he got home, Mum was sitting at the little table under the tree. She beckoned to him. "Come and sit down, Zain. Bring another glass."

He dropped his bag and obeyed, sitting opposite her. She filled his glass from the jug of lemonade in front of her. "Mrs Sharyar called and told me what happened," she said gently.

Zain shrugged uncomfortably. "It's embarrassing."

"No, it's not, Zain. It's part of your journey. You're not on your own, you know." She reached over and patted his hand. "Mrs Sharyar said there is a space for your story whenever you feel ready to tell it. Or not. It's your story, after all."

Zain jumped as a hand dropped on his shoulder. He had not heard Dad approach. He looked up.

"Okay, Zain?" asked Dad.

Zain could tell by the way he looked across at Mum that she had told him what had happened, and he shrivelled inside. Dad would hate such a public display of weakness. He stared hard at his glass as Mum got up and went inside, squeezing Dad's arm as she passed.

Dad took her seat and leant forward. "It must have been hard to have that happen with everyone looking at you," he said unexpectedly.

Zain looked up in surprise.

"I remember being your age, you know." Dad cleared his throat and looked down at the table. "When I arrived from Iran at the age of ten, all I wanted was to be like the other kids at school. Even today, I can forget that simply hiding your weakness is not the same thing as strength." Zain heard the apology behind his words. "If you can go back to school on Monday and just keep going . . ." Dad shook his head. "You'll make me very proud, Zain."

Eleven

Zain's Story

The weekend passed quickly, and before Zain knew it, the boy with skinny legs and a baggy t-shirt was looking back from his mirror on another Monday morning.

This time, though, the boy had a different expression on his face. He looked steady. Calm. Determined.

Once at school, he hung around outside class for a long moment before taking a deep breath and following the other kids inside. Mrs Sharyar was already there, smiling at the jostling students as they shouted greetings to her and each other. Her smile stayed on Zain for a questioning second, before deepening and moving past him.

Once everyone had settled, Mrs Sharyar raised her hand for attention. "People! I want to thank you again for the honour of hearing your wonderful stories last week. A round of applause for you all!" She clapped, and the class joined in with drumming feet and whistles. She held up a hand for silence. "This is our last week together and I want to make the most of it. Today, I want to talk about –"

"I have a story," said Zain.

Every head swivelled towards him. His heart thudded and his breath shook, but he looked steadily at Mrs Sharyar. She nodded, as if unsurprised.

"I have something to say," he said, and it did not even matter that his voice gave a funny squeak.

He got to his feet and walked to the front of class. The ground did not open and swallow him. The sky through the window was still blue, and the trees outside continued to breathe carbon dioxide in and oxygen out. He turned to look at the class and saw that they were just separate people in a room together. *There's no such thing as a crowd*, he thought suddenly. *It's just – individuals in their own heads. There is only ever one pair of eyes looking at me at a time.*

The thought was such a revelation that he blurted out, "Ever since I can remember, I've been afraid of people looking at me." The class went very still.

"Which is a problem," he went on, "since my biggest dream is to hear the applause of an adoring audience." He stopped to catch his breath, to still his thudding heart, and to his surprise, some people laughed. As if he had told a funny joke.

"And then – something happened last week, and I've been thinking about it and my fear of being looked at, a lot." He took a deep breath. "And so, here's my story."

"One springtime, a stray seedling popped its head above the earth into the most beautiful garden. Instead of being happy to grow in such a spot, the seedling looked down at his own plain green stem and worried that he was not worthy of such a garden.

'I don't have the scent of that rose, or the colour of that bougainvillea, or the fruit of that orange tree, or the bright green leaves of that hibiscus,' he thought to himself. 'I don't even know what I am, but I don't belong here. I can't have all these plants looking at me; I'm not nearly lovely enough.'

And so, the little plant did the worst thing that a little plant could do – he hid under a stray leaf that had fallen from the big tree above him. Now, nobody could see the little seedling, but also no sun could reach him, and he needed sun to grow.

Little by little, the little shoot became paler and weaker. His new green stem was now yellow and drab, which made him more determined than ever to hide from the healthy, flourishing plants around him.

Finally, the little shoot was so weak that he lay down on the ground underneath his leaf. 'It's lucky I never showed myself to those other plants,' he thought, limp from sun starvation. 'Imagine how they would have mocked me. It's a good thing that I hid.'

Then one day, a gardener came. He pruned, watered and raked the garden, dragging the leaf off the little shoot.

'Hello, what have we here?' he said, and bent down to look at the little shoot. 'Not looking too healthy, are we? Let's see what we can do about that.'

And the gardener cut back the tree above so that sun could reach the seedling, and fed it some fertiliser. 'You're a little olive plant!' said the gardener.

'Oh!' said the seedling hopefully. 'Will I grow into something beautiful?'

'You will grow into a knobbly, stumpy tree with small, dull leaves and bitter, dark fruit,' said the gardener.

The little seedling bent in shame, but the gardener went on, 'And you will be the most useful plant in this whole garden of lovely fruits and flowers. You will produce precious olives and oil for many years to come.'

And the little shoot realised that his dull green stem was unique and worthwhile, after all, and that he had a place in this garden with all the rest. He stretched out in the sun and was proud of being exactly who he was. A knobbly little olive tree."

Zain looked around the silent classroom. "So, maybe it's a bit babyish," he finished lamely, but the clapping had already begun. More than one of his classmates quickly wiped their eyes as they smiled at him. A jangle of bracelets told him Mrs Sharyar had joined in the clapping, too.

"Bravo, Zain! Your allegory has taken us straight to a great truth. And there is nothing babyish about allegories, or fairy tales, or fables – no matter what some grown-ups might say." She flickered a wink at Zain. "The greatest storytellers have used them for centuries. We have a fondness for them. And I will add another layer to your allegory: this classroom is that garden and *all* your stories are precious, different plants. May they continue to grow for many years – for we need them all."

On Friday afternoon, Zain trudged home with a heavy heart. Today had been Mrs Sharyar's last day, and the prospect of returning to school next term without her laugh, her colour and her stories was a gloomy, grey cloud rolling in after weeks of sunshine. He had said farewell with the rest of the class, and he was sure he was not the only one with a lump in their throat.

He heard Mum talking to someone outside as he closed the front door behind him. His heart gave a leap. Mum had not had someone over for so long! Perhaps it was the nice neighbour.

A laugh like a magpie and a clatter of bangles told him otherwise. He ran to the back door and stared at the impossible sight of Mrs Sharyar sitting drinking tea with his mother. His teacher waved merrily at him, and his mother leaned back in her chair, looking happy and relaxed.

"But – you were just at school," he said in confusion. Had she *flown* here?

"It's such a relief to be freed from doing only what is deemed *possible*," she said with one of her winks. "Now that I'm no longer your teacher, I don't have to obey all the rules."

She was talking in her riddles again. Zain shrugged and laughed.

"Zain, Mrs Sharyar has given us the most beautiful gift," called Mum. She held up a red leather book embossed with gold geometric shapes.

"*The Arabian Nights*," read Zain.

"A very old copy, from around the beginning of last century," said Mrs Sharyar. "I have collected many copies since they were first written down, for sentimental reasons, but I think the ones in Arabic are not as useful to you!" She patted the book affectionately. "This is just one volume of several, but I hope it helps you remember what we learned in the last two weeks, Zain." She looked at Mum. "And you, too, my dear Orla. Make sure you send the school those pictures, won't you? They're in desperate need of a good art teacher. And now, I must fly."

His teacher enveloped him and Mum in a hug scented with cinnamon, saffron and something sweet and smoky.

"Will we see you again?" asked Zain, a bit unsteadily.

"Life is long, Zain," she said. "Who knows what comes next? Whenever you tell a story, or listen to someone tell theirs, I'll also be listening.

I can promise you that." She smiled her big smile. "But now I have other stories to tend to."

With a last jangle of bracelets, she waved goodbye and turned to go inside.

"I'll show you out," called Zain. "Wait, Mrs Sharyar!"

He hurried after his teacher, but by the time Zain got inside, she was nowhere to be seen. Zain ran to the front door and peered outside. It did not seem possible that she was already out of sight – but maybe she had been moving faster than Zain had thought.

Maybe.

Zain slowly turned and went back to where his mum was still standing outside. Mum had opened the red leather book and was looking at a page with a thoughtful expression on her face. Zain stood next to her, and together they looked at the picture of Scheherazade in glossy colour on the inside front page. She had long dark hair piled on her head, a richly coloured headscarf, dangling earrings and a bright, forthright expression that was very familiar.

Her hands were out of sight, but Zain knew without a shadow of a doubt that they would be adorned with bracelets – and that they would jangle with her every move.